The House on tl

Written and illustrated by Clarajane Lewis

www.fast-print.net/store.php

The House on the Hill
Copyright © Clarajane Lewis 2012

ISBN: 978-178035-399-9

All rights reserved

No part of this book may be reproduced in any form by photocopying or any electronic or mechanical means, including information storage or retrieval systems, without permission in writing from both the copyright owner and the publisher of the book.

The right of Clarajane Lewis to be identified as the author of this work has been asserted by him in accordance with the Copyright, Designs and Patents Act 1988 and any subsequent amendments thereto.

A catalogue record for this book is available from the British Library

An environmentally friendly book printed and bound in England by www.printondemand-worldwide.com

This book is made entirely of chain-of-custody materials

To all those who have picked me up when I fell down.

Thank you xx

And out of their houses
the people had run
to stare at the house:
what on earth could be done?

What is the problem?
What could it be?
It makes us quite worried-
we must go and see.

But the village of people were not all that brave so they all went back home- that is, all except Dave.

Now Dave wasn't smart and he wasn't that strong but he certainly knew when something was wrong.

Although he felt scared by the volume of sound Dave opened the door, and inside he found...

A bear and a monkey, a rabbit and mouse, were living together in the small wooden house.

And although as a rule they all got along...

It wasn't uncommon...

for things to go wrong!

Because Bear would get angry and make lots of noise.

And Monkey just hated to share all his toys.

Rabbit was sad and gave a great sigh,
he felt so unhappy he wanted to cry.

Then, as Dave looked around
in the corner he saw
a small worried mouse
curled up on the floor.

'My goodness', Dave said
as he walked through the door.
He gave Rabbit a pat
and took Mouse by the paw.

'I know', he said gently
'why you cry, scream and shout-
you have powerful feelings
you need to get out.'

'But worry you shouldn't, your feelings are good.
It's just that at times they get misunderstood.'

'Now Bear, you feel angry and you really get mad, but that doesn't mean that your feelings are bad.'

'Anger is strong
and you need a safe place
to get it all out
and to do it with grace.'

And out of his pocket
Dave pulled a big box
with a big tube to shout in
and several strong locks.

Then Dave turned to Rabbit
and wiped off his tears.
Poor Rabbit had sadness
that had been there for years.

'Sometimes', Dave said kindly,
'life seems to hard to handle.
Look, here are some tissues
and a bright burning candle.'

'We all have some sadness
it's only quite right,
but never lose faith
in your hope that burns bright.'

'We often have things
which are special and dear,
and it's perfectly natural
to keep them all near.'

'So take all the toys
that give you most pleasure
and put them all here
in this trunk that says TREASURE.'

Then Dave turned to Mouse who was trembling with fear for all of the things that are never quite clear.

'Uncertainty, change
and the things we don't know.
What will they be?
How will they go?'

'Worries are heavy
and weigh us right down.
To let some of them go
will get rid of your frown.'

So with that Dave produced
a bottle of bubbles,
and into the air
floated most of the troubles.

High on a hill on the edge of a lake
stands a small wooden house
with no reason to shake.

The bear and the monkey
the rabbit and mouse
are happy together
inside their small house.

Because they now know
they have ways to feel good,
and that feelings aren't bad-
just misunderstood.